A COLLECTION OF ORIGINAL SHORT STORIES

BY

KADE W FRANCIS

Copyright © 2023 Kade W Francis.

All rights reserved. No part of this book may be reproduced, stored, or transmitted by any means—whether auditory, graphic, mechanical, or electronic—without written permission of both publisher and author, except in the case of brief excerpts used in critical articles and reviews. Unauthorized reproduction of any part of this work is illegal and is punishable by law.

ISBN: 979-8-89031-375-1 (sc)
ISBN: 979-8-89031-376-8 (hc)
ISBN: 979-8-89031-377-5 (e)

Because of the dynamic nature of the Internet, any web addresses or links contained in this book may have changed since publication and may no longer be valid. The views expressed in this work are solely those of the author and do not necessarily reflect the views of the publisher, and the publisher hereby disclaims any responsibility for them.

THE EWINGS PUBLISHING

One Galleria Blvd., Suite 1900, Metairie, LA 70001
(504) 702-6708
1-888-421-2397

THE TABLE OF CONTENTS

THE ACKNOWLEDGMENT v
THE DEDICATION vii
THE PREFACE ix

THE LITTLE BOY 1
THE DOLL 3
THE COW AND THE GOAT 5
THE KITTEN 7
THE CHRISTIAN FAMILY 11
THE BOY AND THE BOOK 15
THE LITTLE PLAY HOUSE 17
MIMI THE PIG 19
THE SNOWMAN 21
THE LITTLE GIRL AND THE MOON 25
THE GIRL AND THE BEANS 27
JIMMY AND THE BALL 31

MR. BELL AND HIS LITTLE CAR	35
KATIE AND THE CAT	37
THE BOY AND THE CLOWN	41
MR BILLY GOAT	45
THE LITTLE FLOWER GIRL	47
THE LITTLE SCHOOL BUS	51
JANE AND HER BOTHER	53
THE BEACH BOY	55
BILL AND HIS FIRST JOB	59
THE TOWN OF BEAMON AND THE STORM	61
NANCY'S DREAM OF DANCING	63
THE BOY GOES FISHING	65
THE MAN AND HIS BOAT	67
AUTHOR'S BIO	69

THE ACKNOWLEDGMENT

I would like to thank my publisher Ewings Publishing, LLC for their help in taking my book to the next level, my Acquisition Manager Pure Roberts for all the information she provided me throughout the beginning stage of the submission process, my Fulfillment Office Anne Reid and all the other Ewings Publishing employees that work on my book to make it a marketable product.

THE DEDICATION

I would like to dedicate this book to my children, James, Jennipher, Jonathan, and to all my grandchildren, to my Mother; who has been an inspiration to me all my life and to my wife who has been there encouraging me throughout the writing of this book.

THE PREFACE

In the past, now, and in the future, children have wanted, want, and will always want someone to read them a bedtime story. It is also a fact that children and adults like to read for entertainment. After a while the same old stories become boring, creating a need for fresh new stories.

It has always been a passion of mine to write short stories, but I could never find the time. Now that I have written this collection of short stories, I hope children and adults alike will enjoy them and consider them as fresh, new, and entertaining for some time to come.

THE LITTLE BOY

There was this little boy that lived with his parents in a small house located in a country town. The boy attended a small one room school that had a teacher who cared a lot about her job and that little town.

The boy's father worked as a locksmith and his mother took care of the house and the children. The little boy had two sisters and two brothers of which he was the youngest of all.

One day the boy went to school as he did each morning and found that his teacher looked sad. "What is wrong Teacher?" ask the boy. The teacher told the boy and the rest of the class that she had received word that her father was ill. The class showed their concern and started to sing a song to cheer her up. The little boy went home and told his parents about his teacher's father.

The little boy's father went into the community and raised money so that the teacher could visit her father. During the time that the teacher was away, the town was praying for a speedy recovery. The teacher returned to the little town and reported that her father was doing much better and thanked the community for what they had done.

When Father's Day came, the town led by the little boy, held a celebration and named the teacher's father as the Honoree.

THE DOLL

There was a little girl who always wanted a doll like the one her best friend own. Due to limited money, her mother could not afford to get the doll for her. You see, her mother has to work two jobs just to provide for them.

The mother would tell the little girl the same thing every time she asked "I cannot get it right now, but some day God will make it possible." Every night before the little girl went to sleep, she would pray for her doll. As she lay in bed, she would imagine herself playing with it.

One day the little girl's Uncle came to visit. There was no school the next day, so the little girl's Uncle took her to the movies. On the way back, they passed a store with the most beautiful doll in the window. The little girl told her Uncle that she always wanted a doll, and would he please buy that one for her. He did and they then took the doll home.

The little girl was so happy, she thanked her Uncle. When they got home, she showed the doll to her mother. The mother thanked her brother for buying the doll, and then said to her daughter, I told you that one day God would make it possible.

She then asked her brother, why he did not check with her first. Her brother replied that he did not think she would mind and asked if his niece could keep it. The little girl's mother said, as the doll make her happy, she could keep the doll, however in the future he should check with her before buying anything. Her brother promised that he would.

When the little girl went to bed that night, she thanked God for answering her prayers.

THE COW AND THE GOAT

On this little farm there was some kind of disease that was making all the animals sick. All the cows died except for one and that one cow moped around because he did not have anyone to play with.

The farmer did not have the money to buy more cows, and he did not know what to do. He went around seeing if any of the neighbors had an extra cow he could have but no one did. He tried to obtain some cows on a "get it now, pay later" plan, but that did not work.

One day a goat wandered onto the farm and noticed that the cow was looking as if he needed a friend. The goat walked over to the cow and asked him what was wrong. The cow replied that all his friends had died and that he had no one to play with.

The goat told the cow that he would play with him. The cow thanked the goat for the offer, but said that it is not the same because he was not a cow. The goat told the cow that he may not be a cow, but he can be his friend and play with him.

From that day the cow and the goat became friends and played all over the farm. The farmer was so glad to see his cow so happy again.

THE KITTEN

There was this family which was made up of a man, his wife and his son. The son kept asking for a brother or a sister because he felt lonely and wished he had someone to play with him. The nearest relatives lived miles away and only on special occasions the little boy and his parents would visit one of the relatives. This was not what the little boy wanted; he wanted someone at home to play with every day.

One day the little boy came home and asked his parents for a pet. He was told at first that he could not have a pet but the little boy continued to ask and told his parents that he would like to have a cat as a pet. His father told him to give them a few days to think about it. Then one day he came home with the cutest kitten the little boy had ever seen.

Before he gave the kitten to the little boy, he told him that he would have to take care of the kitten. The little boy agreed. The little boy played with the kitten which he named Spotty because she was yellow with black spots.

One night the father was lying on the couch with the lights off, watching the TV. All of a sudden he saw a streak pass across his eyes that scared him. It was Spotty running around the house getting into things.

One day Spotty got hold of a ball of yarn that belonged to the little boy's mother and dragged it all over the living room. The mother was upset and told the little boy that he had to get rid of Spotty and he could not have another pet until he got older.

The little boy went to his father crying and told him what his mother said and asked his father to talk to his mother. The father and the mother sat down and had a talk about the little boy and Spotty.

After the talk the little boy's father told him that he could keep Spotty but he would have to keep her from getting into things.

THE CHRISTIAN FAMILY

Once upon a time there was a man, his wife, his son and his daughter who were frequent Church goers. The man and his wife were such strong believers in the Almighty God that the members of the community would call on them to pray for their family members who got sick.

The children would always talk about Jesus to their friends and invite them to Church. *"God Loves You"* is a phrase that the family, use a lot. The family participated in many of the Church's activities. The man is a member of the church board and his wife is a Sunday school teacher.

The family spent a lot of time going to the hospitals praying for the sick and to the jails praying for the inmates. Many individuals came to know the Almighty God and accept Him as their Savior through the efforts of this family.

One day there was a terrible accident in the town. One of their neighbors got seriously hurt in the accident. The doctors did all that they could do, but it did not look good for their neighbor.

All of the family members of the neighbor went to the home of the Christian family, and asked them if they would go to the hospital to pray. The man asked all of the adults that came if they believe there is a God and if He has the power to heal. All but one said yes and the man began to consult with that one. He read scriptures after scriptures until the one was convinced that there was a God then they all left for the hospital.

When they got to the hospital the neighbor was still in a coma. He had been in a coma for a few days. The Christian family began to pray with the neighbor's family in agreement. They prayed for several hours before he showed any improvement. After several days he was completely healed.

After that experience, all the neighbor's family members that were not baptized (adults and children) got baptized and began praying for and with others that they would accept the Almighty God before it is too late.

THE BOY AND THE BOOK

Once upon a time in a little town called Melba, there lived a boy who could not read. His father or his mother would read him a story every night before he went to bed. That boy would pray every night before he lay down, that someday he would learn to read.

One day the Mayor of the little town of Melba hired a teacher to teach reading. The boy, when he heard the news, was so excited that he could not wait to go to the classes. The day came to go to the first class, and the boy woke up early that morning. He went to the class and found that there were several other children in the town that could not read.

The teacher began the class by teaching the alphabets, the vowels and the nouns. Every day the boy went home and practiced what he learned that day.

The boy's father promised him that upon the completion of the classes he would buy him a book. On the way home from the class, the boy would pass the local book store, look into the window and wish the day would come so he could pick the book his father would buy.

The classes lasted for several weeks. Finally the day came! The boy could not wait to go home and read to his parents. His father was so delighted with the little boy's reading; he immediately took the boy to the bookstore.

When the boy and his father returned home, he read the book to his mother and father. The boy loved that book very much because it was the first book he ever owned. He would take the book whenever he visited his friends and read it to them.

Every year on his birthday, the boy's father would buy him a new book.

THE LITTLE PLAY HOUSE

Once upon a time there was a boy and his sister who lived with their parents a few miles from the town. They were what you will call; Country folks. The family raised chickens, goats and pigs that they sell to the town folks.

The work that had to be done was more than the children could stand because it did not leave them time for play.

One day the father called the children to a meeting in the living room. He told them of an idea that he had. He said that because they were such good children, he would build them a tree house. The children would have to promise though, that they would not spend all their time up there. They were so delighted with the idea that without hesitation they agreed.

After the tree house was built, the children would take turns going up into the little play house. They would take their toys up there to play with. When they had homework, they would go up into the play house to be alone.

One day the boy invited one of his classmates to come play with him in the little play house. The classmate's mother brought her son over to the home of the boy and when she saw that the little play house was in a tree she took her boy back home.

MIMI THE PIG

Jake is a farmer that raises several farm animals with pigs being one of them. There was one pig they called Mimi. She was very playful. Mimi would run around the yard chasing the chickens and the ducks. All the animals on the farm loved Mimi because she was so unpredictable.

Jake would take Mimi to the country fair and one year she actually brought home the ribbon. Jake was so proud of Mimi that when they got back to the farm he gave her a special meal. Some of the farm animals got so jealous of Mimi; they would not play with her any more.

After a while she got so lonesome that she would sit by herself and weep. Jake tried to cheer her up by telling her a story, but that did not help.

The day of the fair came once again but Jake could not get Mimi to go. The other animals notice how down Mimi was, that they went over to her and told her if she go to the fair, when she return they would play with her. This made Mimi so happy that she stood up and told Jake that she was ready to go to the fair.

Mimi did not won the ribbon this year but she did not mind, because she knew that she could go back to the farm and play with her friends. When Mimi and Jake got back to the farm they found that the other animals planned a party for Mimi. Mimi in her joy ate and played until she fell asleep.

THE SNOWMAN

Johnny Bench was a 12 year old boy who always wanted a Christmas tree. Johnny's parents could not afford to buy a Christmas tree and all the things that would be needed to dress it up.

One night when Johnny went to sleep he had a dream that a Snowman came to visit him. This new friend of Johnny's talked to him all night long. They would talk about Christmas and what it means.

Mr. Snowman (as Johnny called him) told Johnny that as his parents could not buy him a Christmas tree, he should go out and pick one. Mr. Snowman told Johnny not to pick a big one and not to pick one that is too small, the best rule of thumb is not to pick one that is taller than he is.

Mr. Snowman explained to Johnny that every good thing does not come from a store. There are lots of good things out there in nature.

The next morning Johnny asked his father if he would take him to pick a tree in the forest. His father told him he will but it would be up to Johnny to find the things to dress it up. After Johnny and his father came home with the tree, Johnny went to different stores and asked the store owners if they had any old decorations he could have.

Johnny took these decorations home and using his imagination dressed up the tree. Johnny and his family were so proud of the tree that they invited their neighbors to see it.

When Johnny went to bed that night he once again was visited by his friend Mr. Snowman. He thanked Mr. Snowman for his advice; then told him that because of him, he would have a Merry Christmas.

On Christmas Day when Johnny went outside there was a snowman on the front lawn. Johnny was so happy to see the snowman he called out his family and told them that Mr. Snowman was really here. His mother asked him what is he was talking about and he told them about the dreams he had been having.

They all laugh and then his mother told him, you see what the Lord can do.

THE LITTLE GIRL AND THE MOON

Once upon a time there was this little girl who lost one of her legs in an accident. She was a lonely girl because no one would come to play with her because she only had one leg.

One night while she was lying on her bed weeping, she looked out her window and saw the Moon looking at her. "Why are you weeping little girl?" asked the Moon. The little girl replied, "I lost one of my legs in an accident and now no one would come to play with me because I only have one leg. I have no friends."

The Moon said to the little girl, "If they were your true friends, they would not have stop playing with you simply because you now only have one leg. I will be your friend." Then the Moon started to make faces and bounce around in an effort to cheer the little girl up. This made the little girl laugh and feel happy. She thanked the Moon and said, "Yes, we will be good friends."

The next morning the little girl told her mother about her new friend and her mother told her that it was just her imagination.

Every night since then when the little girl goes to bed, she would look out the window for the Moon. They would play together until she fell asleep, and the little girl was never sad again.

THE GIRL AND THE BEANS

There was a little girl who lived in a small farm house. She had two older brothers and a baby sister. Her father worked long hours on the farm and her mother take care of the home and the children. The older three children attended the small school located in the center of the town. It was such a small town that one individual served as the Police Chief, the Fire Chief, the Judge and the Pastor.

Attending church on Sunday mornings was a ritual for the people who lived in and just outside the town. The Mother would cook beans every Sunday with the meal. Beans were not the little girl's favorite, so she would not eat them. Her mother would try to encourage her to eat the beans and her father would talk to her about how good the beans were. This did not work. She still would not eat the beans. Her brothers even tried making fun of her, figuring this would get her to eat the beans. That did not work either.

One night the little girl went to sleep and had a dream about beans. In her dream, a fairy spoke to her about magic beans. The fairy told her that when she ate the beans, they would perform magic in her body. She will be able to do things that she would not be able to do otherwise.

The little girl asked the fairy what kind of things she would be able to do. The fairy explained to the little girl that she would be smarter in school; she would be able to tell what someone is thinking and would be able to see in the future.

The little was so excited with what she was told by the fairy, that from the next Sunday she would eat all of her beans. Her parents and her brothers all would ask her why the sudden love for beans, but the little girl would not tell them about the dream.

She would tell what her brothers were thinking before they could say anything. Her brothers would try to confuse her by thinking one thought and then saying they were thinking something else. But each time the little girl would explain to them what they were doing. She could also predict the weather. Her mother told her that she was more accurate than the weatherman.

In school, she started making better grades. Her teacher was impressed with the increase in her grades and asked her about her sudden enthusiasm. But just as she didn't tell her family about her dream, she also didn't tell her teacher. She simply said with a slight smile that she studied more.

JIMMY AND THE BALL

Once upon a time there was a boy name Jimmy who always wanted a ball. Jimmy's parents were poor. His father worked in the mail room for a large company and his mother worked for a maid service company. The family was struggling to make ends meet, so there was no money for anything that was considered unnecessary. Jimmy would pray and hope that one day he would own a ball.

One afternoon on his way home from school, Jimmy helped an old man across the street. The old man sensed that there was something troubling the boy so he asked Jimmy what was on his mind. Jimmy told the old man that he always wanted a ball, but his parents were too poor to get him one. The old man told Jimmy that if he wanted a ball so badly, he should find a way to get it himself. Jimmy asked the old man what he meant by that, and the old man told Jimmy to think about it.

For days Jimmy would think about what the old man said and pray about it. One day it came to Jimmy what the old man was trying to tell him - he could earn the money to buy him the ball. There was no business that would give Jimmy a job because of his age, so he would have to do odd jobs on his own.

Jimmy spoke to his parents about what the old man had told him and what he had decided to do. They told Jimmy that they would not object, but they had two stipulations (1) that he would not do anything that is illegal and (2) that it did not interfere with his homework. Jimmy agreed with his parents stipulations and went to his room.

The next day after school Jimmy went to all the neighbors to ask if he could take out the trash or any other thing he can do to earn some money. By the time Jimmy got home he was tired and had only earned about a third of what the ball cost.

The next day was Saturday and there was no school. Jimmy ate breakfast, did his chores at home and then went out into the neighborhood again. Jimmy ran errands, raked the yard, took out trash, walked the dogs and washed cars. By the end of the day Jimmy had made more than he needed to buy the ball he wanted.

With the money that was left, after paying for the ball, Jimmy gave it to his father to help with the house expenses. Every day after school Jimmy and his friends would play with the ball.

One day the kids from another neighborhood were passing by and saw Jimmy and his friends playing with the ball. They ask if they could join the game and Jimmy said no. They told Jimmy that if they are not allowed to play they would take the ball.

Jimmy grabs the ball and ran into the house and told his father what happened. Jimmy's father went out into the yard and told the kids to leave, or they would leave him no choice but to call the Police. The kids from the other neighborhood left and had never seen or heard from after that.

MR. BELL AND HIS LITTLE CAR

Once upon a time a man by the name of Jack Bell lived in a small town and drove a little car. Mr. Bell ran a small general store. He would use the little car to pick up supplies for his store and groceries for his home. The little car served Mr. Bell well for some time, then one day the little car started giving problems. Mr. Bell looked under the hood to see if he could detect what was wrong. He checked and checked, but he couldn't tell what was wrong.

Mr. Bell then walked a few miles until he came to a service station. Mr. Bell told the mechanic working there that his car had stopped a few miles down the road and he could not find what was wrong. The mechanic's name was Mr. Brown, and he called Mr. Blue who has a tow truck. When the tow truck arrived at Mr. Brown's Service Station he told him that Mr. Bell's car had stopped a few miles down the road. Mr. Bell and Mr. Blue went to pick up the little car.

When they got there Mr. Blue hooked up the little car to the tow truck then they drove back to the service station. After looking at the little car for about an hour, Mr. Brown told Mr. Bell that he couldn't find anything wrong either. Mr. Bell asked Mr. Brown, what caused his little car to stop if nothing is wrong. Mr. Brown replied that the little car was tired and needed some rest. He suggested that Mr. Bell take his car home and let it sit for about two weeks, after that it will be fine.

Mr. Bell did what was suggested. At the end of the two weeks, the little car drove like before and that made Mr. Bell very happy.

KATIE AND THE CAT

Katie was 6 years old and lived in a country town. Time and time again, the little girl would tell her mother that she would like to own a cat. So, on Katie's next birthday, her mother got her a kitten and told her that she would have to take care of the kitten and train it to use the litter box. The little girl was so excited to finally have her own cat. She promised to follow her mother's instructions.

Katie named the little kitten Fluffy because it looked like a ball of fur. In the beginning Katie took care of Fluffy. She would give Fluffy a bath, make sure there was food and milk at all times and trained Fluffy to use the litter box. Katie would read books on how to take care of cats and talked to the neighbors that owned cats. Katie and Fluffy would play around all afternoon when she came home from school. Then one day, Katie's mother sat her down for a talk. Katie's mother told her that she noticed that she was spending more and more time with Fluffy and less and less time doing her homework. Her mother told her that school is more important than Fluffy and if she did not get her priorities straight, she would leave her no choice but to get rid of Fluffy. Not wanting to lose Fluffy, Katie started to do her homework. Katie would come from school, have a snack, do her homework; then play with Fluffy until dinner time.

As time passed, Fluffy got older and Katie got even more homework as she moved into higher grades. Fluffy was a very playful cat—running around the house, knocking over things and getting into things. Katie would have to clean up the mess Fluffy made. Katie complained to her mother that between homework and taking care of Fluffy, things were getting too much for her. Her mother gave her two suggestions: one was to get rid of Fluffy and the other was to put Fluffy in a cage when she wasn't playing with her. Katie wanted to keep Fluffy, so she tried the second suggestion.

That was the perfect solution and then all lived happily ever after.

THE BOY AND THE CLOWN

Marcus always wanted to see a circus. He read books about circuses and rodeos, and hoped to see a real one someday. His father always told him that if one ever came to town, he would take him to see it.

One day when Marcus went to school, he saw a flier on the bulletin board that said a circus was coming to town. He got so excited; he couldn't wait to take a copy home to show his father. After school, Marcus ran all the way home. As he rushed through the door, he was shouting to his dad that a circus was coming to town! His father came out from his den and asked Marcus to repeat what he said a little more slowly this time. Marcus handed him the flier, then reminded him of his promise to take him to the circus. His father looked at the flier for a moment, looked at Marcus then told him a promise is a promise. Marcus could hardly wait and when he went to school the next day, he told everyone that he would be going to the circus. It was all he would think and talk about, and because of this, his father also could not wait either.

Finally the circus arrived in town, and Marcus could not sleep the night before. When they got there, everything was exciting to Marcus but he was most taken up with the clowns. Marcus asked his father if he could visit with clowns when everything was over. His father told him that he would see if that is possible. At the end of the show, they went to the Ring Master and asked him if they could meet the clowns. The Ring Master said that he did not see why not, and took them to see the clowns.

Marcus told the clowns that he enjoyed the show very much and they all replied that they were glad to hear that. Then one of the clowns told Marcus and his father how he became a clown. The story was so fascinating to Marcus that he told his father that he wanted to be a clown. When Marcus and his father got home, his father sat down with him to talk about becoming a clown. He told Marcus that being a clown may be a lot of fun but he would prefer for him to go to college. Marcus told his father that he really wanted to be a clown rather than go to college. His father explained that going to college while he is still young would be a plus for him. His father went on to say that after college if he still wanted to be a clown he would then try his hand at it and have something to fall back on if it didn't work out.

Marcus told his father that he understood what he was saying. He then thanked him, hugged him; then went to his room thinking about his day at the circus.

MR BILLY GOAT

Mr. Johnson is a farmer that raises cows, pigs, chickens and goats. He has a special goat that he calls Mr. Billy Goat because he thought the goat was the smartest animal on the farm. All the other animals on the farm would go to Mr. Billy Goat for advice. Mr. Billy Goat would always have a story to tell.

Harriet, the Chicken asked Mr. Billy Goat what he suggested for the pain in her tummy. Mr. Billy Goat told Harriet that there was a special grass that would help her and that she would find it over by the northeast corner of the farm. The farm animals looked up to and respected Mr. Billy Goat.

The other farmers around heard about Mr. Billy Goat and invited Mr. Johnson and his goat to the County Fair. At first Mr. Johnson thought about not taking Mr. Billy Goat to the Fair, after all his goat is not a really show animal. He had never thought to enter Mr. Bill Goat before and wondered if he should do it. The more he thought about it, the more he thought it was a good idea. He decided to take Mr. Billy Goat to the fair.

At the Fair Mr. Johnson and Mr. Billy Goat had a good time attending the festivities and making new friends. Mr. Billy Goat won two Blue Ribbons: one for being smart and the other for the best looking goat.

When they return to the farm, there was a celebration. Mr. Johnson give them extra feed and his wife bake them a cake. All the animals sat around as Mr. Billy Goat told them all about his exciting day at the fair.

Mr. Johnson had a good time as well. He decided he would take more of his animals to the next fair.

THE LITTLE FLOWER GIRL

Once upon a time there was this little girl who lived in a big city. Both of her parents had good jobs and they all lived in a big house in a nice neighborhood. The little girl's name was Bettie and her mother was a lover of flowers and had a lovely flower garden. Bettie grew up helping her mother in the garden and had a love for flowers herself. She would go to school with flowers in her hair and to c.hurch with flowers in her hat. Bettie's mother would put the flowers in her hair in different ways and everyone would complement Bettie on how good her hair looks with the flowers in it. It came to a point that if Bettie did not have her flowers, she would not feel dressed up enough, and she became known as the Flower Girl.

When Bettie's class had an activity, she would provide all the flowers needed with her mother's help. Even their neighbors came for flowers to decorate their tables whenever they had a special dinner for family and friends. Because of her artistic flair with her flowers, one day Bettie's teacher asked her if she wanted to take part in the school's Pageant and Fashion Show. At first Bettie was not sure if she wanted to as she had never done anything like that before.

Bettie went home and talked to her parents about it, and her mother said she thought it was a good idea. Bettie's father told her that it was an experience that many girls dream of and that if she wanted to do it, he would help her in every way, but she had to maintain good school grades. So Bettie decided to participate.

There was much practicing and planning her winning floral design, but Bettie was having lots of fun doing it. The day of the Pageant and Fashion Show came and Bettie felt sure her flowers would help her win. Bettie's parents attended the function and were proud of how good she looked on stage. Bettie won first prize for her original outfit and for the unique arrangement of flowers she had in her hair. On the way home they stopped at one of the fanciest restaurants in the city to celebrate The Flower Girl's win!

THE LITTLE SCHOOL BUS

Once upon a time there was this little school bus that was the children's favorite. The driver of this little school bus was Mr. Green. All the children who ride this little school bus like Mr. Green because he was a nice man. He would talk to the children about the importance of staying in school and gave other fatherly advice.

The little school bus would always be on time to pick up the children to take them to and from school. The little school bus was pretty old but it would still chug along because Mr. Green took good care of it. The children always knew when the little school bus was coming down the street because of the sound it made. The parents felt their children were safe when Mr. Green was driving because they knew that he would take care of them.

One day Mr. Green made an announcement that the little school bus had to go to the shop for repair. During the time the little school bus was in the shop, Mr. Green would use his personal van to take the children to and from school. Those that couldn't fit in Mr. Green's van were taken to and from school by parents.

When Mr. Green got the little school bus out of the shop, he drove it around the neighborhood to let everyone know. All the children and their parents were happy to see the little school bus back on the road.

Mr. Green took very good care of that little school bus until the day he retired.

JANE AND HER BOTHER

Jane had a baby brother named John whom Jane helped take care of. John was a playful little boy. When Jane came home from school, she would have a snack, do her home work; then play with John until he falls asleep.

Jane's mother was happy that she helped her with John, and Jane would tell her mother that she was glad to do it because she loved her brother. John likes when his sister plays with him and when she feeds him.

When Jane's friends come over to the house, Jane would not let them go near her brother. They would look at him from afar and make faces so he would laugh. Jane's friends thought John was so cute they would come over often just to see him and take pictures of him.

As a result of all the attention he got, John grew up very spoiled. Jane and her mother were very sorry for what they did and they discussed what they could do to fix things. His mother decided to enroll John in an all-boys boarding school to learn discipline.

After he went away, Jane and John would call and write each other often, and whenever possible his mother and sister would visit. After a few years, John returned home and they all lived happily ever after.

THE BEACH BOY

Jack, his sister, two brothers and their parents lived in a small house near a beach. Jack didn't get along well with his brothers and sister because he was somewhat different from them. They would play what Jack called silly games and all Jack wanted to do was go to the beach. At the beach Jack would swim, try to catch small fish with his hands, and make sand castles. His brothers and his sister were not too interested in those games. They would prefer to stay home and play, so either Jack would go to the beach alone, or his mom or dad would go with him. His parents wondered why Jack was so amazed with the beach, but didn't question him too much about it. At the beach, Jack would make new friends with other kids who liked the beach as much as he did. Jack spent so much time on the beach, he became known as the Beach Boy.

One day at school, his art teacher gave an assignment where the students would have to make a display of their favorite hobby. Jack thought it was one assignment where he would definitely get an 'A'. After school, Jack walked around the beach and picked up as many of the pretty sea shells he could find. The next day he went to the library and checked out a book on sea shells and read about the different shells he had picked up. When he finished with his project, his brothers and sister saw even more evidence for his nickname Beach Boy and told him he had the best project.

The day for the children to bring in their displays came. All the projects were well done and the teacher was impressed. The entire school came to view the displays. Each student was asked to vote for the project he or she felt was the most creative. At the end of the day, Jack's display received the most votes.

When Jack got home, he gave everyone the good news. His family congratulated him and then they celebrated.... at the beach.

BILL AND HIS FIRST JOB

Once upon a time there was a boy named Bill who lived in a small town called Thomasville. Bill's friend George had just gotten a bike and Bill would ride it sometimes. But Bill wanted his own bike so he asked his father if he could get one. But his father could not afford it.

The next day, Bill told George that his father couldn't afford to get him a bike. George then told Bill that he should do odd jobs like he did to get the money to buy himself a bike. So, with his father's permission, Bill got himself his first job ever at the local grocery store with the owner Mr. Jake. Mr. Jake explained that Bill's responsibilities would be to keep the store clean, take out the trash, run some errands, and he would work two hours after school Monday thru Friday and four hours on Saturday.

Bill's father spoke to him about being a responsible employee, getting to work on time and doing the best he can. And if he didn't understand or know something, he should always ask a question to be sure. Bill started the job and after a few weeks Mr. Jake told Bill's father how pleased he was with Bill's performance.

When Bill got paid he would save half of his pay and give his father the other half to help with the household expenses. It took some time but Bill was finally able to save the money to buy his bike.

Bill continued to work for Mr. Jake and contributes to the household expenses. He would ride his bike to school, then to his job and finally home. Bill loves his bike so much that he would not let anyone else ride it and he would take very good care of it.

THE TOWN OF BEAMON AND THE STORM

There was once a little town called Beamon where most of the residents were very poor. The leaders of Beamon tried to get assistance from the Government to improve their town, but help was slow to come and things were going to get worse.

A storm was going to come right through Beamon, and the residents began to prepare as best they could. The Storm passed through Beamon, and there was a lot of damage to the houses, farm lands and public buildings. This time the Government responded and contractors were sent to build housing. Food, clothing, medicine and other necessities were provided to and for the residents. All the residents, children and adults, of Beamon worked very hard together to get their little town to better than what it was.

It took some time, but Beamon was put together better that it was before. Things got so much better for Beamon that new businesses and new facilities opened up, more visitors started coming to the town, and new families started to move in to the town.

While a storm is a bad thing, as a result of that storm passing through Beamon that day, the leaders of the town declared that day "Beamon Storm Day", where thanks would be given for all the improvements to Beamon.

NANCY'S DREAM OF DANCING

From the time Nancy could walk, she was dancing. She might not have had the rhythm or the balance, but she was dancing! So as soon as they were able to, her parents enrolled her in a dance class. Nancy and her mother went to the dance school to register Nancy for classes.

Mrs. Dole was the instructor and she welcomed Nancy as a student. She explained to them what dancing was all about and what Nancy had to do to become a good dancer. Nancy was a good student and practiced all the time.

Then it was time for Nancy's first appearance as a dancer. She was so excited and nervous at the same time, but managed to give such a good performance, that her parents gave her a standing ovation.

Nancy continued dancing until she started high school – then she switched to playing soccer.

THE BOY GOES FISHING

Chris was a farm boy and an only child. He, his mom and dad always had a lot of work to do on the farm, but at times he and his dad went fishing.

Sometimes they would go on Saturday or on Sunday after they returned home from church. Chris learned a lot of things from his father, but he especially liked what he learned about fishing. Some days they wouldn't catch anything and other days they had to give some fish away to the neighbors.

One day Chris' father got sick and was taken to the hospital. It turned out that his father had a stroke and had to stay in the hospital for some time. Chris and his mom would visit his father as often as they could. With his father in the hospital, he had more work around the farm to do so he couldn't get to fish as he would have liked.

One day some neighbors came and asked him if he wanted to go fishing with them. He didn't want to go because it was something he enjoyed doing with his dad, but he didn't want to make his neighbors feel bad, so he went. While the fishing trip that day was good, it wasn't the same as when he went fishing with his father.

After a few more weeks, Chris' father was doing much better and was released from the hospital. While his dad couldn't do so much around the farm as he used to, he could still fish, and they both went fishing once again.

THE MAN AND HIS BOAT

Once upon a time there was a man named David who lived by himself on a lake in his boat named Ms. Mary. David finds it a peaceful and quiet life.

One day there was a boat show and just to do something different, David entered Ms. Mary in it. At the show, David met Charlie who had a boat exactly like Ms. Mary, only a different color. Charlie was about the same age as David, lived with his wife and two sons, and when he wanted to be alone, he would go on the lake in his boat. They started to compare their boats and good naturedly argued which one would win. It turned out that neither boat won, but they didn't mind. It was enough that they had become friends.

And while at times David and Charlie's family would meet and enjoy each other's company, for the most part, David continued to live his peaceful, quiet life on Ms. Mary.

AUTHOR'S BIO

I am a former bookkeeper, truck driver and businessman living in Arkansas. I have 2 children, 5 grandchildren and 1 great-grandchild.

During my younger years, my mother read to me. As I grew older, I read to her. I was fascinated with short stories and always thought of writing my own. Over the years, I made several attempts but didn't follow through. After some time, I decided to give it a try once again. After I wrote a few stories, my wife at the time, co-workers and friends read them and told me to pursue my dream, so here it is.

Reading is something that will always be enjoyed by children and adults. I hope that the readers of this book find it entertaining, educational, and enjoyable.

I welcome your comments and can be contacted at:

kwfrancis04@yahoo.com

www.ingramcontent.com/pod-product-compliance
Lightning Source LLC
LaVergne TN
LVHW091545070526
838199LV00002B/219